# Sunflower House

## EVE BUNTING

*Illustrated by* KATHRYN HEWITT

Harcourt Brace & Company

*San Diego   New York   London*

Text copyright © 1996 by Eve Bunting
Illustrations copyright © 1996 by Kathryn Hewitt

Library of Congress Cataloging-in-Publication Data
Bunting, Eve, 1928–
Sunflower house/written by Eve Bunting;
illustrated by Kathryn Hewitt.—1st ed.
p.  cm.
Summary: A young boy creates a summer playhouse by planting sunflowers
and saves the seeds to make another house the next year.
ISBN 0-15-200483-1
[1. Sunflowers—Fiction. 2. Stories in rhyme.]  I. Hewitt, Kathryn, ill.  II. Title.
PZ8.3.B92Su  1996
[E]—dc20  95-5422

GFEDC
*Printed in Singapore*

The paintings in this book were done in
watercolor and colored pencil on watercolor paper.
The display type was set in Phyllis and
the text type was set in Spectrum.
Color separations by Bright Arts, Ltd., Singapore
Printed and bound by Tien Wah Press, Singapore
Production supervision by
Warren Wallerstein and Cheryl Kennedy
Designed by Lisa Peters

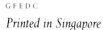

*To Anna Eve*

*We will have tea in your sunflower house*

*——E. B.*

*For John, Cody, and Annelise, who blossomed together*

*at First Pres in Santa Monica*

*——K. H.*

First I pull out all the weeds.
Then I sow my sunflower seeds.

It says to set them in a line
but Dad says round and round is fine.

I give them water every day
and shoo the pesky birds away.
"Go eat the berries on the tree!
These sunflower seeds belong to me."

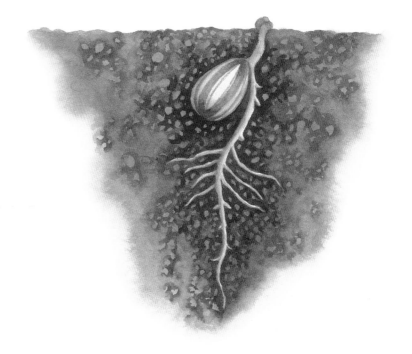

The package says they're guaranteed.
"A mammoth flower grows from each seed."
My friend Bernice says, "There's no way."
"You don't know everything," I say.

"WAIT!"

The stems poke up, all ringed around,
a pale green circle in the ground.

They're growing tall,
they're growing fast.

And—oh my gosh!
SUNFLOWERS at last!

All frilly yellow, big and bright—
mammoth is the word, all right.

Their petals open wide and spread
a golden roof above my head.
My friends come rushing down to see
the sunflower house, hand grown by me.

There's lots of room inside for three.
Mom brings us cookies and iced tea.
But Mom and Dad can't fit at all.
They're much too big and wide and tall.

All summer long the house is ours.
We play in it for hours and hours.
It's a castle, it's a cage,
we're jungle beasts that roar and rage.

My friends sleep out with me one night,
bundled up and snuggled tight.

Moon shadows shiver on the ground.
The sunflowers whisper all around.

They whisper songs of heat and rain
and things too secret to explain.
I see the stars play peek-a-boo
and wish a wish that can't come true.

One day the leaves are tinged with brown.
A flower comes tumbling, rumbling down.
Next day some more bend over, fall.
And now it's not a house at all.

We tie it up with string and sticks,
but it's impossible to fix.

It's gone, there's nothing we can do,
not even with the Glues-All glue.

"WAIT!"

There's still the puffy middle part
that's filled with seeds, enough to start
another sunflower house next spring,
with walls, a roof, and everything.

It's neat to think when something's gone
a part of it goes on and on.
It's such a super-duper plan!
We pick out all the seeds we can.

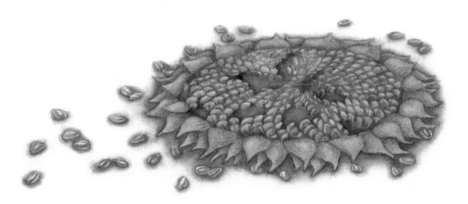

Our pockets bulge.  The bluejays come,
the sparrows, crows; they all take some.

We still have lots and lots to share.
Now be aware. Prepare. Take care.

Next summer they'll be everywhere!!!